S0-AFB-687

This book belongs to

. . . .

Written by Elanor Best.
Illustrated by Stephanie Thannhauser.

RhinO CORN

Elanor Best • Stephanie Thannhauser

make
believe
ideas

Riley believes with all of her HEART that you CANNOT tell her and her BEST FRIENDS apart.

She has a COOL TAIL,
FOUR LEGS, and a HORN.
In **RiLeY'S** view,
she's a UNICORN!

Her meals are all made up of
PINK LOLLIPOPS.

FIZZ-SHERBET TEA,
and SWEET CANDY DROPS.

When racing down RAINBOWS
she knows she will win...

...she PLUMMETS straight down with a big CHEESY grin.

WHEEEE!

One day, as **Riley** was SKIPPING along,
she BUMPED into someone who looked
tough and **strong**.

Her eyes opened wide and
she let out a SCREAM:

"You're the

MOST GIANT

UNICORN

I've ever seen!"

Big Rocky laughed as he boomed,
"That's not true!

I'm not a UNICORN...
neither are you!
We're **RHINOS**, with four legs for **stomping** around.

OH NO!

Our tails **swat** at flies

and our horns
dig the ground."

SEEDS

RILEY thought NONE of those things sounded FUN
and decided to show **Rocky** how things were done.

"Our UNICORN horns
are the COOLEST of things.

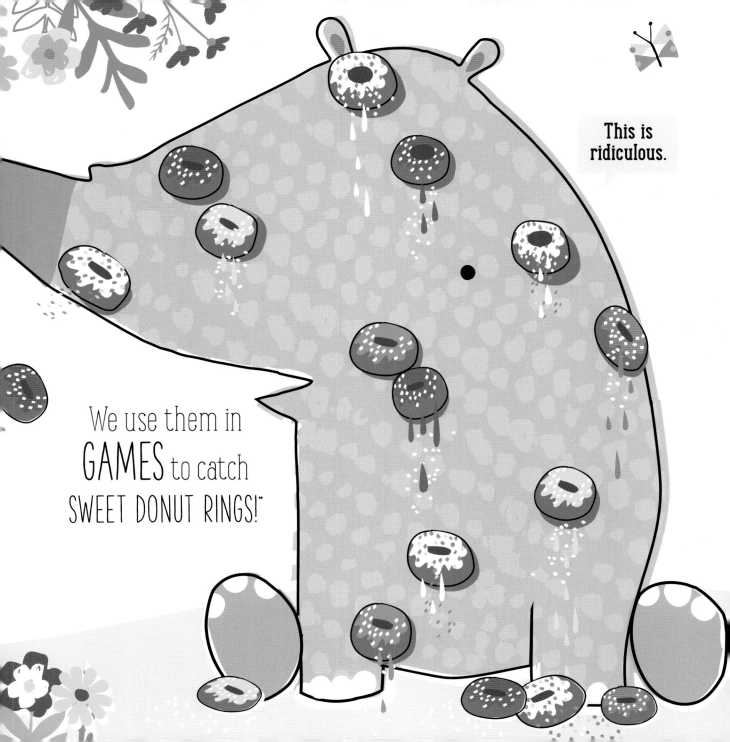

"Our UNICORN tails
are not what they seem.

With a MAGICAL FLICK,
they make RAINBOWS that GLEAM!"

Amazing.

"Our UNICORN legs are for dancing BALLET.
First, POINT your toes, then try a PLIÉ.

So with ALL that in mind,
I think you'll AGREE,

that we are as

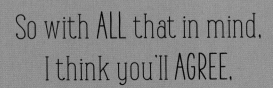

'UNICORN'

as UNICORNS can be!"

Rocky HEMMED and he HAWED
and he SCRATCHED at his head.

"I **think** that you're something **brand-new**," **Rocky** said.

"You LOOK like a rhino with **legs**, **tail**, and **horn**, but you've **shown** me today...

...you're a

Rhino

CORN!

Half-rhino,
half-unicorn,
that's what you are.

You are **true** to yourself,
which is better by **far!**"

Rocky said,
"I've had so much **fun**,
playing with you.
I think that I **might** be
a RhinoCORN too."

Riley and **Rocky** then lived happily,

being as RHINOCORN as RHINOCORNS can be!